Dr. Martin

HELPING YOUR BRAND-NEW READER

Here's how to make first-time reading easy and fun:

- Read the introduction at the beginning of each story aloud. Look through the pictures together so that your child can see what happens in the story before reading the words.

- Read one or two pages to your child, placing your finger under each word.

- Let your child touch the words and read the rest of the story. Give him or her time to figure out each new word.

- If your child gets stuck on a word, you might say, *"Try something. Look at the picture. What would make sense?"*

- If your child is still stuck, supply the right word. This will allow him or her to continue to read and enjoy the story. You might say, *"Could this word be 'ball'?"*

- Always praise your child. Praise what he or she reads correctly, and praise good tries too.

- Give your child lots of chances to read the story again and again. The more your child reads, the more confident he or she will become.

- Have fun!

First edition 2012

Library of Congress Cataloging-in-Publication Data is available.

Library of Congress Catalog Card Number pending

ISBN 978-0-7636-5732-1

11 12 13 14 15 16 SWT 10 9 8 7 6 5 4 3 2 1

Printed in Dongguan, Guangdong, China

This book was typeset in Arta Medium.
The illustrations were done digitally.

Candlewick Press
99 Dover Street
Somerville, Massachusetts 02144

visit us at www.candlewick.com

COOKIE MONSTER'S BUSY DAY

ILLUSTRATED BY **Ernie Kwiat**

CANDLEWICK PRESS

Contents

Cookie Monster Cleans Up

Introduction

This story is called *Cookie Monster Cleans Up.* It's about how Cookie Monster washes the different parts of his body, and then tries to share the soap with Oscar!

Cookie Monster washes his hands.

He washes his face.

Cookie washes his arms.

He washes his belly.

Cookie washes his knees.

He washes his feet.

Cookie gives the soap to Oscar.

"No, thanks!" says Oscar.

Cookie and Elmo Eat Their Colors

Introduction

This story is called *Cookie and Elmo Eat Their Colors.* It's about how Cookie Monster and Elmo eat different-colored foods. Then Cookie eats a rainbow!

Cookie Monster eats an orange carrot.

Elmo eats a red apple.

Cookie eats blueberries.

Elmo eats green peas.

Cookie eats purple grapes.

Elmo eats yellow corn.

Cookie eats a rainbow cookie.

"Me love rainbow color!" says Cookie.

Cookie Monster and the Parade

Introduction

This story is called *Cookie Monster and the Parade*. It's about how Cookie's friends move and travel in different ways. Together, they make a parade!

Cookie Monster walks.

Elmo rides his tricycle.

Abby flies.

Big Bird roller-skates.

Grover rides a skateboard.

The Count rides a scooter.

Zoe dances.

The friends make a parade!

Cookie Monster's Bed

Introduction

This story is called *Cookie Monster's Bed*. It's about how Cookie makes his bed. It's a lot of work, and he gets tired!

This is Cookie Monster's bed.

Cookie puts a sheet on his bed.

He puts another sheet on his bed.

He puts a blanket on his bed.

He puts a pillow on his bed.

He puts another pillow on his bed.

Cookie Monster is tired.

Cookie goes to sleep.